What is phonics?

Phonics helps children learn to read and write by teaching them the letter sounds (known as phonemes), rather than the letter names, e.g. the sound that 'c' makes rather than its alphabetic name. They then learn how to blend the sounds: the process of saying the sounds in a word or 'sounding out' and then blending them together to make the word, for example c – a – t = cat. Once the phonemes and the skill of blending are learnt, children can tackle reading any phonetically decodable word they come across, even ones they don't know, with confidence and success.

However, there are of course many words in the English language that aren't phonetically decodable, e.g. if a child gets stuck on 'the' it doesn't help if they sound it out and blend it. We call these 'tricky words' and they are just taught as words that are so 'tricky' that children have to learn to recognise them by sight.

How do phonic readers work?

Phonic reading books are written especially for children who are beginning to learn phonics at nursery or school, and support any programme being used by providing plenty of practice as children develop the skills of decoding and blending. By targeting specific phonemes and tricky words, increasing in difficulty, they ensure systematic progression with reading.

Because phonic readers are primarily decodable – aside from the target tricky words which need to be learnt, children should be able to read the books with real assurance and accomplishment.

Big Cat phonic readers:
Sam and the Nut

In Big Cat phonic readers the specific phonemes and tricky words being focussed on are highlighted here in these notes, so that you can be clear about what your child's learning and what they need to practise.

While reading at home together, there are all sorts of fun additional games you can play to help your child practise those phonemes and tricky words, which can be a nice way to familiarise yourselves with them before reading, or remind you of them after you've finished. In *Sam and the Nut*, for example:

- the focus phonemes are s (Sam), a (at), t (top), p (picks), i (in), n (nut), m (mad), c (can), g (gets), k (kick), ck (picks), d (dog), e (gets), o (on), u (up). Why not write them down and encourage your child to practise saying the sounds as you point to them in a random order. This is called 'Speed Sounds' and as you get faster and faster with your pointing, it encourages your child to say them as quickly as possible. You can try reversing the roles, so that you have a practice too!

- the tricky words are 'the', 'no', 'to' and 'go'. You can play 'Hide and Seek' by asking your child to close their eyes and count to 10, while you write each word on a piece of paper, hiding them somewhere in the room you're in or the garden for your child to find. As they find each one, they should try reading and spelling the word out.

Reading together

- Why not start by looking at the front cover of *Sam and the Nut* and talking about what you can see.

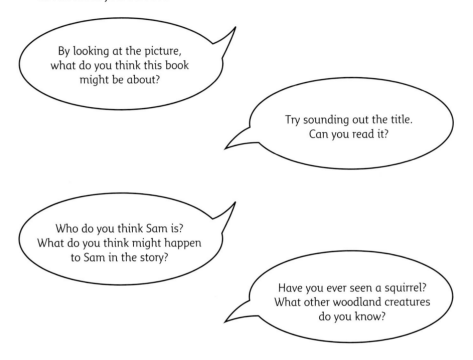

By looking at the picture, what do you think this book might be about?

Try sounding out the title. Can you read it?

Who do you think Sam is? What do you think might happen to Sam in the story?

Have you ever seen a squirrel? What other woodland creatures do you know?

- Enjoy reading *Sam and the Nut* together, noticing the focus phonemes (s, a, t, p, i, n, m, c, g, k, ck, d, e, o, u) and tricky words (the, no, to, go). It's useful to point to each word as your child reads, and encouraging to give them lots of praise as they go.

- If your child gets stuck on a word, and it's phonetically decodable, encourage them to sound it out. You can practise blending by saying the sounds aloud a few times, getting quicker and quicker. If they still can't read it, tell them the word and move on.

Talking about the book

- Use the story map on pp18–19 to retell the story together.
- Practise the focus phonemes from *Sam and the Nut* by asking your child to tell you which sound, for example, the word 'dog' begins with, or how they'd sound out, for example, 'nut'.

Sam
and the
Nut

Written by Sheryl Webster
lustrated by Giuditta Gaviraghi

Collins

The nut is at the top.

Sam can go to the nut.

Sam can go up and up.

Sam can tap the nut.

Sam can kick the nut.

The nut is in the mud.

A cat nips at the nut.

Sam is sad.

A dog picks up the nut.

Sam is mad.

Sam gets the nut.

Go, Sam, go!

A story map

Getting creative

- Have some sticky fun with your child by looking through some newspapers and magazines together and seeing if you can spot any of the focus phonemes from *Sam and the Nut*, cutting them out and making a collage.

- To practise the tricky words from the story, why not play 'Tricky Tiddlywinks', where you write the tricky words down on different pieces of paper, spread them out over the table and play tiddlywinks – aiming at the words. If they land a tiddlywink on a word, they have to read it or even spell it!

- If your child's enjoyed reading *Sam and the Nut* they could try making up a different ending to the story. Maybe a lion could come along and take the nut? Or the nut could roll down a hole? They could draw pictures to illustrate their ending, or write it out using as many of the focus phonemes and tricky words they've been practising as they can.

Other books at Level 1:

Fiction	Non-fiction
Ant and Snail — Paul Shipton, Jon Stuart	Got It! — Charlotte Guillain, Leo Hartas-Roberts
We Are Not Fond of Rat! — Emma Chichester Clark	Pet Cat, Big Cat — Alison Hawes
Sam and the Nut — Giuditta Gaviraghi	Pond Food — John Townsend, Pamela Anzalotti

Collins Big Cat
Reading Lions

Published by Collins
An imprint of HarperCollins*Publishers*
1 London Bridge Street
London
SE1 9GF

Text © 2010 Sheryl Webster
Illustrations and design © HarperCollins*Publishers* Limited 2010
This edition was published in 2015.

British Library Cataloguing in Publication Data
A catalogue record for this publication is available from the British Library.

Illustrator: Giuditta Gaviraghi
Designer: Nicola Kenwood @ Hakoona Matata
Parent notes authors: Sue Reed and Liz Webster

Printed and bound by RR Donnelley APS

www.collins.co.uk/parents